P9-CJL-858

HILLSBORO PUBLIC LIBRARIES
Hillsboro, OR
Member of Washington County
COOPERATIVE LIBRARY SERVICES

WITHDRAWN

Disney MINNIE

A Walk in the Park

Adapted by Gina Gold
Based on the episode written by Jennifer Heftler
Illustrated by Loter, Inc.

SUSTAINABLE FORESTRY INITIATIVE
Certified Chain of Custody
Promoting Sustainable Forestry
www.sfiprogram.org
SFI-01415
The SFI label applies to the text stock

Disney PRESS
New York • Los Angeles

5547 5353 01/15

Copyright © 2014 Disney Enterprises, Inc. All rights reserved. Published by Disney Press, an imprint of Disney Book Group. No part of this book may be reproduced or transmitted in any form or by any means, electronic or mechanical, including photocopying, recording, or by any information sto information address

HILLSBORO PUBLIC LIBRARIES
Hillsboro, OR
Member of Washington County
COOPERATIVE LIBRARY SERVICES

If you purchased this book without a cover, you should be aware that this book is stolen property. It was reported as "unsold and destroyed" to the publisher, and neither the author nor the publisher has received any payment for this "stripped" book.

Everyone is making bows.
The dogs get in the way.

"We cannot work," Daisy says.
"How about a walk?" says Minnie.

"Dogs love to walk," says Minnie.
"Me too," Millie says.

"Look!" says Cuckoo-Loca.
"Hot dogs!"

"I want one," says Daisy.

"Five hot dogs, please,"
Minnie says.

The hot dogs smell yummy.

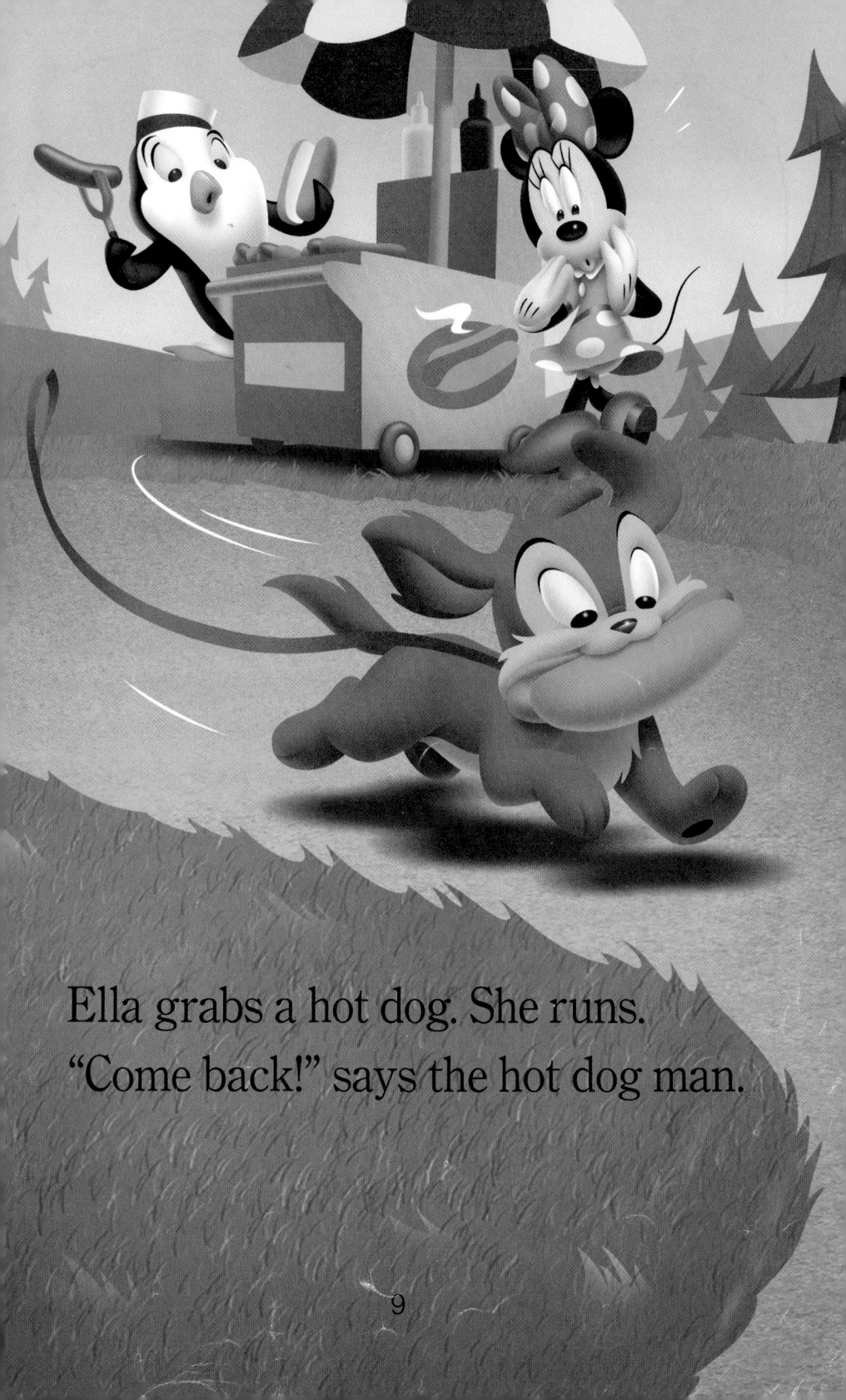

Ella grabs a hot dog. She runs.
"Come back!" says the hot dog man.

"Stop!" the twins cry.

"Dogs on the run!" says Cuckoo-Loca.

"Help me!" says Minnie.

"The dogs run fast!" Minnie says.

"They are over there!"
says Cuckoo-Loca.

Ella jumps.
The ball machine turns on.

The balls bounce.
"Look out!" says Cuckoo-Loca.

Minnie shuts off the machine.
"Time to clean up," she says.

Wait! Ella sees something.
What does Ella see?
She sees a squirrel.

Ella chases the squirrel.
"Slow down!" says Daisy.

The dogs pull Daisy.
"Help!" she says.

"Come on!" says Minnie.
"Daisy needs us."

The dogs keep running.

Daisy cannot stop them.

Daisy goes up.

Daisy swings.

Daisy slides down.

Daisy goes around and flies off.

Daisy lands in the sand.
"Are you okay?" says Minnie.

"We cannot chase the dogs,"
Daisy says.
"It is too hot," says Cuckoo-Loca.

"Hot . . ." says Minnie. "Dogs . . . That's it!"

Minnie has a plan.

"Ready, set, go!" says Minnie.
Hot dogs fly.

The dogs stop to catch them.

"Now," says Minnie.
"We can walk."

Wait! Ella sees something.
What does Ella see?
She sees a cat!

The cat runs. Ella runs.
The dogs run.

"Not again," says Minnie. "Run!"